E
C

K — 1st Grade

The Dirt Road

CAROL AND DONALD CARRICK

THE MACMILLAN COMPANY | COLLIER-MACMILLAN LTD., LONDON

The Macmillan Company, 866 Third Avenue, New York, N.Y. 10022
Collier-Macmillan Canada, Ltd., Toronto, Ontario

Library of Congress catalog card number 73-116758

FIRST PRINTING

To Vener

197 37

A highway runs through our valley,
but I live on a dirt road
that ends in a farmer's yard.

We can hear a car from a long way off.

The road is full of bumps and holes.

The town grader scrapes it smooth again.

I can find the prints of deer hoofs
in the soft dirt near the brook.
Ben and I make our own tracks.

A caterpillar is crawling across
the road. I let him tickle my hand.

In sunny spots the road is hot.
Raspberries grow by the edge.

Watch out, Ben! I'm making it rain dirt.

Cows follow us along the fence.
When we stop they stare.

Ben barks and races down the road.

He tries to follow the rabbit,
but he never catches one.
Dirt sticks on the end of his nose.

A porcupine doesn't have to run away.

Near the farm a pipe runs under the road.
It makes a good hiding place.

There are my friends. They are calling,
"Lunch is ready! Why did you take so long?"